Arielle and the
Hanukkah Surprise

by Devra Speregen and Shirley Newberger
illustrated by Lena Shiffman

Cartwheel
·B·O·O·K·S· ™

SCHOLASTIC INC.

New York   Toronto   London   Auckland   Sydney

Text copyright © 1992 by Scholastic Inc.
Illustrations copyright © 1992 by Lena Shiffman.
All rights reserved. Published by Scholastic Inc.
CARTWHEEL BOOKS is a trademark of Scholastic Inc.

ISBN 0-590-46125-7

12   11   10   9   8   7   6   5   5   6   7/9

Printed in the U.S.A.   24

First Scholastic printing, October 1992

On the day before Hanukkah, Arielle sat at the kitchen table drawing a dreidel. Her Grandpa Judah walked into the kitchen with his arms full of brightly colored packages. Arielle always loved when her Grandpa came to visit. Especially for Hanukkah!

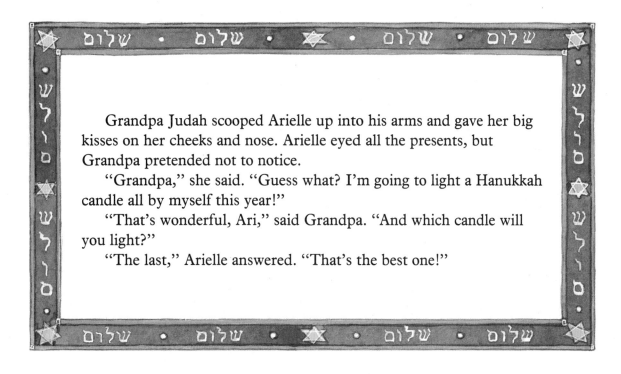

Grandpa Judah scooped Arielle up into his arms and gave her big kisses on her cheeks and nose. Arielle eyed all the presents, but Grandpa pretended not to notice.

"Grandpa," she said. "Guess what? I'm going to light a Hanukkah candle all by myself this year!"

"That's wonderful, Ari," said Grandpa. "And which candle will you light?"

"The last," Arielle answered. "That's the best one!"

"Oh, I don't know about that," said Grandpa. "I think every candle is important. The menorah needs all eight to make it shine so bright and pretty."

"Happy Hanukkah," Grandpa called to the other children.
"I'm staying for the whole holiday this time, all eight nights. I hope
you won't get tired of me!"

"Tired of you, Poppa? Never!" said their mother as she came into the dining room carrying shopping bags filled with gifts.

Arielle noticed that there were more presents than usual. "Oh," she gleefully announced, "I can't wait till tomorrow!"

That evening, after dinner, Arielle searched her room for the special list her mother had made for her. Because there were so many candles to light during Hanukkah, Arielle had a hard time remembering who would light which one. The list was to help her remember.

Arielle found the list under a coloring book and plopped down on her bed to look at it. "Let's see," she said out loud, "there are eight candles and eight people. Daddy is the oldest. He lights the shammes and the first candle. Then Mommy lights the second. Elana and Becka light three and four. Benji and Jared light five and six. Matthew lights seven. Then me. I light the last candle!"

All of a sudden, Arielle remembered Grandpa Judah.

"Oh, no!" she cried. "With Grandpa, there are nine people and only eight candles!"

Arielle felt her face get hot. "Now I won't get to light a candle," she said. "Why can't there be *nine* nights of Hanukkah instead of eight? And why do I have to be the youngest?"

Arielle ran down to the kitchen to ask her mother about the candles. "Not now, Arielle," her mother said. "I'm busy getting ready for Hanukkah."

Arielle went to the dining room to ask her father.
"Not now, Arielle," he said. "It's past your bedtime. The sooner you get to sleep, the sooner it will be Hanukkah!"

Arielle kissed her father good night. She would ask about the candles tomorrow.

The next morning, Arielle's mother was busy frying potato pancakes. The kitchen smelled scrumptious! "Can I have a latke?" Jared asked.

"No, silly," his mother laughed. "You can't eat potato pancakes for breakfast! Hurry up, kids, or you'll miss your school bus."

Finally the first night of Hanukkah arrived. Arielle watched as her Grandpa, the oldest, lit the shammes and the very first candle. Then it was time to open the presents!

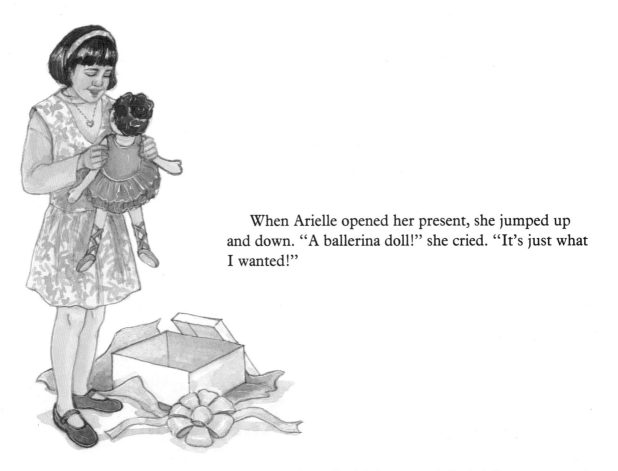

When Arielle opened her present, she jumped up and down. "A ballerina doll!" she cried. "It's just what I wanted!"

That night, snuggled up cozy in bed with her new doll, Arielle forgot all about lighting a Hanukkah candle.

On the fifth night, Grandpa handed the shammes to Becka. Arielle was so jealous! "Can I light this candle?" she asked.

"No," said Becka, "it isn't your turn."

"When *is* it my turn?" Arielle asked.

"Stop worrying, Ari," her father said gently. "Everyone will get a turn to light a candle. Why don't you go open your present?"

Night after night, Arielle waited for her turn to come.
Grandpa Judah led the children in singing the holiday prayer.
Arielle sang, too, but her heart wasn't in it.

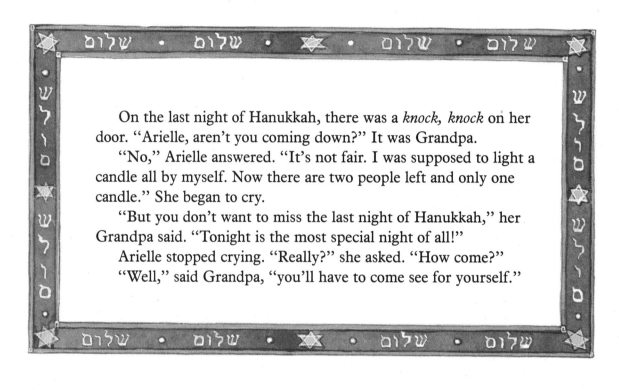

On the last night of Hanukkah, there was a *knock, knock* on her door. "Arielle, aren't you coming down?" It was Grandpa.

"No," Arielle answered. "It's not fair. I was supposed to light a candle all by myself. Now there are two people left and only one candle." She began to cry.

"But you don't want to miss the last night of Hanukkah," her Grandpa said. "Tonight is the most special night of all!"

Arielle stopped crying. "Really?" she asked. "How come?"

"Well," said Grandpa, "you'll have to come see for yourself."

Grandpa wiped away Arielle's tears with his handkerchief.
Then he took her hand and led her downstairs.

On the way down, Arielle noticed that it was
too quiet and too dark. Where was everyone?

Suddenly, the lights snapped on. "Surprise, Ari!" everyone shouted. "Happy Birthday!"

"My birthday?" Arielle asked.

"Yes," answered her mother. "How could you forget?"

Everyone giggled.

"Hanukkah fell on your birthday this year," added Grandpa. "We've been planning your surprise for weeks!"

"Open your birthday present," said her father.

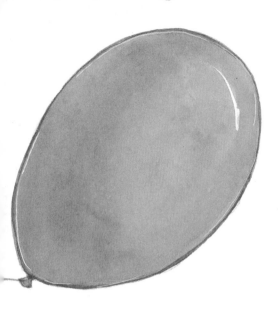

Arielle tore open the box. Inside was a shiny, new menorah!

"Now you can light all eight candles on your very own menorah," Grandpa said with a smile. "Happy Hanukkah *and* Happy Birthday, Arielle!"

At last it was Arielle's turn to light the Hanukkah candles—all by herself.

We say this prayer each night as we light the candles:

Praised be Thou, O Lord	*Ba-ruch a-ta a-do-noy,*
Our God, King of the Universe,	*el-o-hey-nu me-lech ha-o-lam,*
Who has sanctified us with His commandments	*a-sher kid'shah-nu b'mitz-vo-tav,*
And commanded us to kindle the Hanukkah lights.	*v'tzee-va-nu l'had-lik ner, shel Ha-nuk-kah.*

This prayer gives thanks for the miracles that took place on the first Hanukkah. We say it each night, too.

Praised be Thou, O Lord	*Ba-ruch a-ta a-do-noy,*
Our God, King of the Universe,	*el-o-hey-nu me-lech ha-o-lam,*
Who performed miracles for our ancestors	*sher-asa nee-seem la-a-vo-tey-nu*
In days of old at this season.	*ba-ya-mim ha-hem ba-z'man haz-zeh.*